THE MAGIC BABUSHKA

An Original Russian Tale

Phyllis Limbacher Tildes

TALEWINDS
A Charlesbridge Imprint

In loving memory of my aunt,
Catherine Chervenak Simokat,
who taught me the art of pysanky

And a special thanks to my editors, Juliana McIntyre
and Yolanda LeRoy, for their inspiring guidance

A TALEWINDS Book
Published by Charlesbridge Publishing
85 Main Street, Watertown, MA 02172-4411
(617) 926-0329
www.charlesbridge.com

Library of Congress Cataloging-in-Publication Data
Tildes, Phyllis Limbacher.
The magic babushka, an original Russian tale/Phyllis Limbacher Tildes.
p.   cm.
Summary: A gentle, farsighted peasant girl rescues the legendary
Baba Babochka and is rewarded with a magic babushka that enables her
to create beautiful "pysanky," or decorated eggs.
ISBN 0-88106-840-3 (reinforced for library use)
[1. Fairy tales. 2. Easter eggs—Fiction.
3. Vision—Fiction. 4. Russia—Fiction.] I. Title.
PZ8.T48Mag 1998
[E]—dc21   97-14274

Printed in the United States of America
10 9 8 7 6 5 4 3 2 1

The illustrations in this book were done in watercolor and gouache on
Strathmore 4-ply illustration paper.
The display type and text type were set in Berkeley Oldstyle.
Color separations were made by Pure Imaging, Watertown, Massachusetts.
Printed and bound by Worzalla Publishing Company, Stevens Point, Wisconsin
This book was printed on recycled paper.
Production supervision by Brian G. Walker
Designed by Phyllis L. Tildes and Diane M. Earley

Long ago in a distant land, there was
a kind and gentle peasant girl named Nadia.
She lived with her grandfather in a wooden hut,
called an *isba*, on the edge of a birch forest
in the rolling hills of Russia.

Nadia loved animals and all the gifts of nature. When she heard the lilting trill of a bird, smelled a fragrant blossom, touched a downy chick, or tasted a ripe berry, she was happy. However, when she tried to look closely at them, they were blurry. For as long as she could remember, Nadia had been unable to see small details clearly.

Each spring the girls in every village decorated eggs for Easter. The colorfully patterned eggs, called *pysanky,* were blessed by a priest and given to loved ones on Easter morning. At this special time of year, Nadia's imagination was a swirl of beautiful designs that she longed to create on pure white eggs, but the detailed artwork was too difficult for her weak eyes.

One spring the ruler of the land, Tsarina Zoyanna, and her nephew, the prince, announced that there would be a special award for the girl who created the most magnificent basket of *pysanky.* The Tsarina had a passion for beautiful things. Her collection of jewel-encrusted enamel eggs could have paid to feed the entire kingdom for a year.

All the village girls were excited about the contest. When Nadia went to the market, the girls crowded around her, fighting over the flawless white eggs she had brought to sell. They argued over who would transform the eggs into award-winning *pysanky*. After Nadia finished her marketing, she walked back home with a heavy heart.

Nadia's grandfather sat by the hearth waiting for her return. He greeted her with a smile and a gentle touch to her cheek. He could see her tears and knew the reason for her sorrow.

As she prepared some broth for him, he said, "Nadia, you are my precious prize. My hope and prayer is that your own special gifts will bring you happiness." She smiled and kissed his forehead.

The next morning,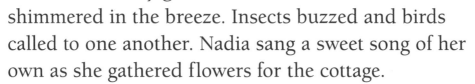
as the warm spring sun
awakened new life in the
woods, Nadia went to look for
wildflowers. Tiny green leaves
shimmered in the breeze. Insects buzzed and birds
called to one another. Nadia sang a sweet song of her
own as she gathered flowers for the cottage.

Entering a thicket of brambles, she came upon a
horrible sight. Caught in the web of a poisonous spider
was a delicate fluttering butterfly. As the spider closed
in on its prey, the butterfly struggled helplessly to free
itself. Nadia could not bear to see such a beautiful
creature suffer. She plunged her hand into the web to
free the lovely insect, then placed it carefully on a tuft
of moss. The butterfly rested for a moment. Slowly it
fanned its wings, which began to glow brightly. To
Nadia's amazement, the butterfly grew larger and larger
as it gradually transformed into a little old grandmother
wearing a babushka on her head.

Nadia recalled the legend of the butterfly woman,
Baba Babochka. Long ago her magical powers were the
envy of an evil Tsar, who tried to force her to use her
magic for cruelty and war. Instead, she turned into a
butterfly and fled to the peace of the deep forest.

Nadia's eyes were as wide as poppies when she asked, "Are . . . are you Baba Babochka?"

"Yes, my lovely girl, I am. You are the first person to see me in many years." The old woman smiled at Nadia. "Do not be afraid, my little one. You were indeed brave to save me from that spider's snare. I will reward you with one wish, but it must be something for yourself alone. You must not tell anyone that you saw me or my magic, or I will lose my power to transform. Now, take your time and choose wisely," warned Baba Babochka.

But Nadia was so excited, she said the first thing that came into her mind. "I wish that my imagined *pysanky* were real."

"Very well," said the old woman as she removed the colorful kerchief from her head. "Take this magic babushka and wrap your finest white eggs in it. Set them in the moonlight, and in the morning you will find that your wish has been granted."

Early the next morning, Nadia unwrapped the eggs in the corner of the *isba* where the moonlight had shone. Nestled in the folds of the babushka were bright and intricately patterned *pysanky*. Even with her weak eyes, Nadia could see that the eggs were embellished with her own imagined designs. She wanted to show them to her grandfather and the village girls but thought they would ask too many questions. Everyone knew she could not see well enough to produce such beautiful work. Why had she not asked Baba Babochka for perfect vision? "How stupid I am," thought Nadia. "No wonder I was warned to choose wisely."

Just then there was a knock at the door. Nadia quickly hid the eggs in a crock and opened the door. Standing in the morning light was a handsome young man holding the reins of his horse.

"Good morning, maiden," he said. "My horse has been injured, and I need fresh water and a salve for her wounds."

Nadia hurried out to attend to the deep scratches on the visitor's horse, while the young man bragged to her grandfather about his riding adventures. He strolled around the cheerful cottage filled with pots of wildflowers and the aroma of freshly baked bread. Through the window he could hear Nadia humming a simple tune.

He noticed the earthen crock on the table. Hoping to find something to eat, he lifted the lid. He was amazed to see the beautiful *pysanky* instead. He knew he would be in trouble when he returned home late, so he thought a special gift might appease his aunt. Making sure no one was looking, he carefully placed the eggs in his satchel.

"Nadia, our guest must be hungry," said her grandfather as she entered the cottage. Blushing, she offered him some warm bread. After devouring most of the buttered *kalach*, he thanked them both and rode away with the carefully concealed eggs.

This young man was none other than Tsarevich Dmitri, the nephew of the Tsarina. Having no child of her own, she chose to raise him after the death of her younger sister. However, the young heir had grown into a headstrong, spoiled prince. As usual he had disobeyed his aunt to go riding without an escort.

Tsarina Zoyanna was indeed furious at the prince until he showed her the extraordinary eggs. All morning she had been receiving *pysanky* from the girls of many villages, but none were of such quality. Anxious to meet the artist, she summoned the peasant girl to the palace at once.

Clippity clop, clippity clop . . . the hooves of galloping horses shook the *isba* as the royal coach approached. Timidly Nadia opened the door. "Her imperial majesty, Tsarina Zoyanna, requests your presence," announced a stern palace coachman. Nadia was stunned. She embraced her grandfather and climbed into the coach. "What could I have I done wrong?" she wondered as the carriage raced toward the palace.

The coach left her at the palace gates. Nadia was led up steep marble stairs and down a long corridor to the royal throne room. She trembled as she approached Tsarina Zoyanna and Tsarevich Dmitri. Not only was she shocked to learn that the brash young man she had met was the prince, but there he was, holding a golden bowl filled with her *pysanky!* The Tsarina was an imposing figure in her jewels and headdress. "I am amazed at your skill. You will be awarded a special place in the palace as my court artist. But first you must demonstrate your art."

Nadia was terrified. Her only desire was to have wished more carefully that day in the woods. Although she wore the magic babushka, she could not show how its magic produced *pysanky*. She had promised Baba Babochka.

Nadia was taken to a room prepared with baskets of goose eggs and bowls of colorful dyes. The Tsarina ordered her to begin. Holding a wooden stylus in her shaking hand, she heated the metal tip in the candle flame and filled it with hot wax. Struggling to see, she tried to draw fine wax lines on the curved surface of the egg. When Nadia dipped the egg in the vibrant dyes, clumsy designs appeared. The Tsarina was furious.

The prince suggested that Nadia might be hungry. As he smiled on encouragingly, a sumptuous meal of caviar, blini, borscht, and smoked salmon was served. Nadia politely ate the delicacies, but still she could not create a beautiful egg. The prince thought that Nadia might need soothing music to relax her. But even the melodies of the finest court musicians could not help her weak eyes.

The Tsarina was enraged. "You are an impostor!" she shrieked. "You could not have made these *pysanky*. Who did?" Before Nadia could speak, the prince assured his aunt that he himself had seen Nadia create the *pysanky*. He suggested that she was tired and needed rest.

At that the Tsarina turned her anger on Tsarevich Dmitri. Tired of his lies and mischief, she ordered him out of her sight. Shaking her finger at Nadia, she said, "Tonight you will sleep in the tower. You will have one more chance in the morning. Show me that my nephew is not lying about your skill or you will be imprisoned until I find the true artist."

Alone and afraid in the tower, Nadia wondered what to do. She was angry that the prince had stolen the eggs and angry with herself for having made such a foolish wish. What good was the magic babushka if she could not use its magic? . . . Or was there some way she could?

Nadia put the magic babushka over her head and tried to make herself disappear. Nothing happened. She knotted it into the shape of a butterfly and waved it out the tower window, hoping to signal Baba Babochka for help. But the old woman did not appear. She tied the babushka and her bedding to an iron hinge outside the window, hoping to climb down, but it was still too far to the ground. In despair she wept, wiping her tears with the babushka.

As the sun began to set, a butterfly flew through the window. Nadia called out, "Is that you, Baba Babochka?"

Once again the wise old woman appeared. Nadia was relieved to see the ancient grandmother and quickly explained her predicament. Baba Babochka took Nadia's hand in hers and said, "You are a good girl and have kept your promise. However, tears will not help you see clearly. You yourself have the answer to your problems. You have many gifts. Use what has been given and in the morning you will see what you will see."

With that the old woman hobbled to the window, where the setting sun framed her hunched form as it started to glow. She turned into a butterfly and flew away.

Nadia pondered Baba Babochka's words. What were her gifts? She had a sweet voice, a great love for nature, and a vivid imagination. And of course she had another wonderful gift—the magic babushka.

As Nadia undressed for bed, she softly sang a prayer her grandfather had taught her. A curious mouse came out of its hiding place. Smiling at its twinkling eyes and twitching whiskers, Nadia offered it a bit of bread that she had saved from the feast. After eating the morsel, the mouse washed its face, covering its eyes with its paws. This gave Nadia a wonderful idea. She made a blindfold out of the babushka, tied it around her eyes, and lay down on her cot in the silver moonlight. Soon she drifted off to sleep dreaming of beautifully patterned *pysanky*.

In the morning Nadia untied the babushka and opened her eyes. She looked at the detailed designs of roses on the kerchief. She looked at the tiny black spots of a ladybug sitting on the windowsill. She could see everything perfectly!

When the smiling girl was brought before the Tsarina to try her skill once more, the real magic began. The prince and his aunt watched with amazement as Nadia's nimble fingers and sharp eyes created delicate designs on the surface of the eggs. Before long she presented a basket of exquisite *pysanky* to the Tsarina. Surprised and pleased, Tsarina Zoyanna embraced her nephew and proclaimed Nadia the award-winning artist.

That Easter was very special for Nadia and her grandfather. They celebrated Holy Week in the palace, where the priests blessed her beautiful *pysanky* and her Easter *kulitch* cake. On Easter Sunday, she presented one of her finest eggs to the prince.

In the years that followed, Nadia's artistic ability and fame grew, as did the prince's admiration for her. In time, he changed from a headstrong youth to a kind and patient man.

Their growing friendship blossomed into love, and with the Tsarina's blessing, the couple were wed. Upon the death of Tsarina Zoyanna, Dmitri and Nadia became the rulers of a happy kingdom.

Russian Words

baba (BAH-bah): woman

babochka (BAH-botch-kah): butterfly

babushka (bah-BOOSH-kah): scarf or kerchief. Literally, babushka means "grandmother" and is pronounced "BAH-boosh-kah." When you pronounce it "bah-BOOSH-kah," it also has come to mean the kerchief that many old peasant women wear.

blini (BLEE-nee): pancakes

borscht (BORSHT): beet soup

isba (EEZ-bah): hut or cabin

kalach (kah-LAHTCH): a kind of white bread

kulitch (koo-LEECH): a sweet Easter cake

Nadia (NAHD-yah): nickname for Nadezhda (nah-DEZH-dah), meaning "hope"

pysanky (pee-SAHN-kee): patterned eggs decorated using dyes and wax

tsarevich (zar-AY-vitch): prince

tsar (ZAR): emperor

tsarina (zar-EE-nah): empress

Pysanky comes from the word meaning "to write," as the designs are actually "written" on the egg with a tool called a stylus that is filled with hot beeswax. The egg is then dyed in consecutively darker colors. Down through the centuries, the people of Eastern Europe have celebrated spring by transforming the common egg into a thing of beauty. With symbols of stars, crosses, wheat, flowers, birds, fish, and animals, *pysanky* artists celebrate life and rebirth as they decorate eggs for their families and loved ones.

In Ukraine, where the art of *pysanky* was perfected, it was believed that the fate of the world depended on the number of *pysanky* made each year. Evil, in the guise of an ancient, vicious monster chained to a cliff, would be unleashed if too few *pysanky* were made. If they were plentiful, the monster's chains held tight, allowing love to conquer evil.